BETRAYAL TO SUCCESS

BLIND FAITH

PRERNA SINGH

Made with ♥ on the Notion Press Platform
www.notionpress.com

My Parents are the biggest source of inspiration for me Today and always. They have always wanted me to be self-made. I am setting a new milestone for myself by writing my books today.

I have a lot more to achieve in life. I want my DAD in heaven to be very proud of me.

Contents

Preface

My journey from a housewife to an author has been very long. started writing in bits and pieces. They wrote on blogs and apps like Pratilpi, momespreso.

My confidence was boosted and I decided to write my book.

ONE

"WRONG DECISION "

"Jhanvi wake up, wake up quickly you have to accompany me to college today",

Rohit was pushing her wife Jhanvi hard to wake her up.

"What's the time? Are we very late Rohit?

Sorry, I don't know when I fell asleep again", Jhanvi woke up in a hustle.

"No issues, just get ready we still have an hour", Rohit replied calmly.

Jhanvi had woken up at 5 for her mother-in-law. She had left for Varanasi. She cooked her complete meal for the train. She insisted on homemade food. Managing everything she finally left at 8. Jhanvi was exhausted and slept on the sofa reading the newspaper.

Rohit is a Sr.Lecturer in the university college. Today they had a family reunion, and everyone had insisted on bringing Jhanvi. He never prefers taking her along anywhere. Shyness, inferiority complex,...

In an hour Jhanvi was ready in pink chiffon saree. Her long black curly hair dazzled on her back. She had curious blue eyes which got magnified with kajal.

Anybody who meets her never forgets her smiling addictive face. She is the epitome of beauty. Rohit was wheatish colored handsome man in his early thirties. He too had a magnetic personality. But yes Jhanvi was just amazing from a different world altogether. They left for the college and reached there on time. The moment Jhanvi entered the college premises everyone was mesmerized with her beauty. Jhanvi just recalled her First day in college.

Kashmira came running to meet Rohit. She was his colleague and often flirted with him. She just stumbled on the floor, looking at Jhanvi. "Take care, Kashmira. Why are you running? " shouted Rohit. He was a little embarrassed by her actions.

"Hi all I am Jhanvi Dixit. Rohit's better half. It's so good to meet u all today. Rohit keeps talking about all his students and fellow Friends. Look today I have the opportunity to meet you all. It's gonna be fun."Jhanvi was so excited to be back in college after 8years.

"Oh Jhanvi comes here", a mild voice of an old man came from behind.

"Juneja Sir, you are still here. I asked Rohit so many times about you but he never responded", Jhanvi bowed down to touch his feet.

"You are still the same Jiny", said Juneja sir with tears flowing from his eyes.

"What are u doing these days .. you must be DM now. You had the dream to be an IAS officer", Juneja had a spark in his eyes.

Jhanvi was shocked that her mentor still remembered her dream. But with time and Rohit's obsession with me, today I realize where I have reached in the last eight years. There was a flashback in her eyes. Sister Agatha had come for her admission in 2005. She was the first child of the orphanage who had qualified the engineering with great marks. College was very big and Sister Agatha was very worried she insisted on meeting the principal.

Mr. Abhinav Juneja read the nameplate outside the office.

We waited for a few minutes and then we were called inside. He was in his fifties and became very impressed with my accomplishments. He became my guardian and promised Sister Agatha to be my mentor forever.

I stayed in Juneja sir's home for the next 4 years with his family. It was the most wonderful period of my life.

I met Rohit Dixit who was in my batch and like all the girls of the college I was impressed with his intelligence and attractiveness. You can say it was my first crush. Both of us passed out from this college 8years back as college toppers.

Just after graduation, Rohit joined the college as an ad-hoc. It was then he offered a marriage proposal to Juneja sir and Sister Agatha. Sister Agatha was very happy but my mentor disagreed. He wanted Jiny to live up to her dreams and be the person he wanted to be.

Juneja sir was completely against the decision of so early marriage of Jhanvi. But she was too curious to marry Rohit and have a family. She had always been in the orphanage so going to Ina family was her biggest dream.

Finally, soon after college, I got married and moved to Rohit's house. She had a younger sister and mother. Everyone was very loving but soon I realized that Rohit

was not the same .....

My mentor was right I had made a wrong decision.

TWO

"BETRAYAL"

6th August 2009 results were announced and Jhanvi had topped the school and even the university. Rohit was second but in boys, he had also topped. She was on top of the world. She had cleared the TCS test also and had been offered for Chennai. Everything she had dreamt of was on her feet today. Juneja sir and Sister Agtha were watching there Jiny spreading happiness and zeal to work hard. Rohit took his trophy and left for home. He said his mother was very ill and won't coming for the evening get-together. Jhanvi's magic was everywhere. In the evening she was dressed in a white satin gown with no makeup up and still, she mesmerized everyone. All girls and boys want to be around her. Dance, games, catwalk, ramp .... Everything happened.

Finally, our college was over, I was super excited for the new beginning. My sacrifices and hard work had been answered. I had been teased by friends and classmates that I was a bookworm, boring, and a LOST case. That was my "FOCUS" on my goal to be the topper. For me, college life was an opportunity for my successful life. For others, it was fun-filled classes, friends, canteen masti, traveling, and what all you were not allowed in school life. Today I was standing at height above them all with the brightest future for myself. There were a few others as well who had made it through interviews and had offers in hand. But most people were still stressed about what to do ahead.

Today I ponder why Rohit was not selected. Maybe he was always overconfident. He did instant studies and scored well in exams. But when it came to cracking interviews and entrance he always failed.

Jhanvi had a one-sided love for Rohit. But she had never disclosed. Few of her friends knew about it. But it was never serious because for Jhanvi career was the most important. She joined TCS and stayed in Chennai for around a year.

One day Juneja sir called her and asked her to pay him a visit on her next vacation. After 2 months she came to meet him. He had retired as the Principal but still gave lectures.

"Rohit wants to marry you. He visited me twice and has requested to convey his proposal to you", said Juneja sir seriously.

He seemed to be worried.

"What Rohit !!", Jhanvi said shockingly.

Never in her wildest dream had he imagined.

"But how I have never spoken to him. We have just been batchmates. And in the past year never had an opportunity to talk or meet", exclaimed Jhanvi.

"I know, even I am surprised with his sudden proposal. But he insisted on meeting you once. He wants yes/no from you. This is a serious matter and I don't want you to be in a rush to decide anything".

"Hmmm, I am not getting it", Jhanvi was still in shock.

" no issues Jiny go and get fresh. Will be waiting for u for dinner. Your aunty has prepared chicken tikka ur favorite", smiled Juneja sir.

Jhanvi retreated into her room thinking about Rohit. Every memory revolved in her mind sitting behind him to see his glimpse, in the library peeping through the books, on weekends following him to restaurants... so many stupidest stuff.

She laughed at herself and got ready for dinner.

Together they enjoyed dinner like college times. Chitchat with Juneja sir was never-ending. Finally, at 12:30 we moved to our rooms after getting scolded by Aunty.

There Jhanvi lay straight on the bed watching the fan going round and round. God had made me an orphan, but he blessed me with a beautiful life with people like sister Agatha, and Sir. My hard work was answered and got the best job in college. And today love my life was approaching to marry me. How could I thank you God? When I dozed off I don't remember.

Jhanvi woke up with a knock at my door.

"Just a moment", she shouted.

I quickly brushed my hair and managed my dress. It was Rohit.

Jhanvi pinched herself hard thinking as if she was daydreaming. No, it was him. In a white shirt and denim jeans. Hairs properly gelled back.

" I am too desperate to meet you and propose", he suddenly sat on his knees.

"I want to marry you Jhanvi. I love you from the bottom of my heart", he raised his hands with a small diamond ring.

Jhanvi had no words. She was frozen as if daydreaming. In excitement, she held out her hand to wear the ring.

Yes, she shouted and they hugged each other. They moved down the dining hall to meet Juneja, sir. Seeing them together he understood, that what he was afraid of had come true. But Jhanvi was an adult and knew what was best for her. She had commitments with TCS for another 8 months. So marriage was fixed after that in September 2011. With time their love bloomed and flourished. Finally, the Big day was here and in a very simple private ceremony, they married. Rohit's mother Karuna was a very simple and sober person. She was a window and mostly devoted her time to God. Her sister Priya was in 12th grade. She loved Jhanvi so much. After marriage Soon they left for Honeymoon.

In the valley of Srinagar, their bond became stronger and Rooted. After a month they got back to their daily routine. Rohit was ad-hoc in college with a salary of 30k pm. Jhanvi got promoted in TCS and got her new posting in Banglore with a 7lpa package. She was super excited. Everything she had wished was with her. Karuna blessed her and left for the Ganga Sagar tour. She was mostly on pilgrimage. Rohit dropped her at the airport and left for the office.

After 2-3 days she got a call that Rohit had met with an accident. Jhanvi reached home. At that time there was no work from home. He had severe leg damage and was bedridden for months. Jhanvi left her job and took care of Rohit. In a year and a half, everything got routine. Jhanvi was unable to understand how to ask Rohit if she wanted to join back.

She met Juneja, sir, "Hello sir, how r you? Need your opinion." Said Jhanvi politely.

"Yes, Jinny tell me, what's the matter? You sound serious." Juneja sir lifted his head.

" I want to join back work, but how to ask Rohit", she said with a sad face.

"You need permission to resume your work. But why whole life you have worked hard to be a successful working woman? Today you want permission?

I don't understand Jiny why are you doing this to yourself? I told you before also you could have kept a nurse for Rohit, but you have wasted more than a year. And now you want permission", he was very disappointed and furious at Jhanvi's sudden decision.

" I thought everything emotionally sir. But I will surely get a new job. I promise next time I will be here with my offer letter." She promised and left in a rush. She worked hard to crack interviews and Rohit made certain plans for travelling. He would say for so many months sitting in one room was ridiculous. Jhanvi could not say NO.

Time flies and it was 3 long years she had not cracked any interview. She didn't have the confidence to meet Juneja sir. Jhanvi cleared technical always but HR rejected saying you have commitment issues. Once you have taken family over work. In the future, if head a project and some family issues happen you will again leave. Now her routine was cooking, cleaning, and looking after Rohit and her mother.

Soon Priya cleared her graduation and her marriage stars were shining. Time was running out of hand and I felt it was my destiny. It was 2016 now and I had a long gap. All my savings were on the verge of ending. Priya's marriage was all at my expense.

Came back to the present day. Meeting Juneja sir has filled my confidence back. It seems I am incomplete without my own identity.

Rohit and his gang were sitting in the garden having the on-the-rocks party. I stood there watching Rohit like I used to in college. Suddenly there was great applause in the garden. She moved a little closer to hear the conversations. And to her surprise

"So I have won the challenge, all of you owe me 20k. Transfer the amount right now to my account."Rohit was bossy

"Yes, we salute your strategy you have made college topper your maidservant". Loud laughter burst into the room.

"It's unbelievable how Jhanvi agreed to marry you and then leave her career", again a big laugh and clapping followed.

What I was a part of the challenge. Rohit wanted to let me down just because I was ahead of him. Better in every way. Juneja sir's worst dream was true today. Jhanvi rushed to her room. She cried all night. Rohit slept in the guest room with his friends. She was unable to understand how she ruined herself.

She was *betrayed.*

THREE

"PREPARATION FOR REVOLT"

In a few days, Jhanvi was back as strong and confident girl as she used to be in college. Her only goal in life was to stand on her own feet and get a financial backup for herself. Rohit had ruined her career and was living a lavish life on her savings. Everything Priya wanted in marriage was given by Jhanvi. It was her love for the family, but now. She had been taught a lesson of life. Never trust people easily. Meeting family like Juneja sir she had thought the world was kind and loving.

Nobody had cared for her as much Juneja sir.

She prepared hard and even took classes for herself. Night and day she just focused on her dream.

Rohit was busy with college exams and then the university election. He never paid heed to what I was doing. I am portrayed as if I am still his puppet. Wasting her life for him and her family.

Although Priya and Aunty never objected to me and loved me as much. Aunty never forced me for anything what I want wear, what I wanted to eat. My sleeping and awakening time. She was truly a spiritual lady.

But now I had chosen my path.

Finally, the result day was here. My heart was pounding like hell.

I told Aunty I was going to visit Juneja sir and would be back after dinner. I informed the same to Rohit as well.

Reached the cafe and checked my result.

I closed my eyes and joined both my hands. There it was Jhanvi Dixit district topper.

Yeah, I shouted and jumped on my seat. My hard work was answered I qualified for UPSC on the first attempt.

Yes, you hear me right my aspiring dream was true. I hurried to Juneja sir's house with a printout. He was sitting in the garden having evening tea. I took samosa and jalebi. He was super excited to see his Jiny. I gave him his spectacles and asked him to read the paper.

For a few minutes he jingled to study but he too jumped from his chair and hugged me.

Tears flowed from his eyes.

"U made it my dear u made it."

Juneja sir was so very proud of me. They had no children and when sister Agatha brought me they adopted me as their daughter. They provided me with everything for my education and comfort. They never forced their opinion on me.

They mentored me on the right path but waited for me to make a move. A true mentor who guided me with his enlightenment.

" I wanted to see this day before I die my Jiny and thought you had lost all ur confidence. But see you surprised me again".

We had a few discussions about the interview and he promised to come with me.

I left for home. My home. I felt like an orphan again with no home.

Rohit was waiting at the dining table for me. He had sweets in his hand.

For a moment I felt he got the news too early.

But then he said I am promoted as the HOD today for my department. I ate his sweet and moved towards Aunty to touch her feet.

"I also want to share some good news with you both. I was not confident at first but now when I have cleared..."

Rohit disrupted my conversations.

"You don't need to look for a job now Jhanvi, I have a revised salary now of 3-4 lac and even a small apartment on the university campus." Said Rohit proudly interrupting my conversation.

I said nothing and gave the printout to Aunty.

"District UPSC topper. God bless you Jhanvi. You are extraordinary with excellence in all fields, being women managing everything. I am so proud that you are my daughter-in-law."

She hugged me tight and straight away went to make Prasad to offer god.

I waited for Rohit's expressions.

He was in shock and couldn't believe his eyes and ears.

"When did u appear for upsc and when you prepared."

"Night and day I was preparing for the same. You were too busy with college and friends. Never bothered about me and my whereabouts."

"Overconfidence of destroying someone's life makes you blind with illusion"

Saying this I moved to my room and accompanied Aunty in the kitchen. Her happiness was so pure. She asked about my interview and how when I be traveling. I informed her that Juneja sir would accompany me.

Soon the news was all over. Everyone came personally to congratulate and even the mobile kept buzzing endlessly. The whole sitting area was filled with bouquets and flowers.

I again thanked God for his blessings.

When I came into my bedroom, Rohit was sitting in my study and was silent.

"Did you know about my real motive to marry"

" yes I do long back on the family reunion day I overheard your win over me", I replied.

"This is my answer to your victory"

I closed the light and went to bed.

Rohit was awake the whole night.

Morning he left early for college.

Aunty arranged Dhawan for me and invited some close relatives and neighbors. Even Juneja sir came with their wife.

Aunty loved me by heart.

Rohit had changed completely neither did he talk much nor showed any arrogance.

My interview date has come and left for Delhi with my mentor. I was selected as an IAS and posted in Nagpur.

Last time I went to Rohit's house to get all my things. He was nowhere to be found. Aunty had prepared ladoo, mathri, gud ke paare and whatnot. Aunty knew all my needs. She blessed me to attain great success and promised to come soon to stay with me.

Priya was also the reason she brought a beautiful purse for me.

I never had any grudge for them. We talked and discussed the future. I insisted they visited me often.

I, Juneja sir, and Aunty left for Nagpur. In the next fortnight, we were all busy settling our daily lives.

Slowly office workload was also given to me. Everything came to routine in 2 months. Juneja sir was here to stay with me forever. Their health and my loneliness both were well taken care of ...

Time passed and no sooner it had been 8 months. It was my birthday.

Early morning doorbell rang it was Rohit, with bouquets of roses.

I was unable to understand, how to react.

We were not divorced and neither of us thought over it. Just there was this period of silence, long 8 months.

We met over breakfast. Juneja was happy to see him. I left for my office without a word. Evening well I returned late and sir and man had slept already.

"I am sorry for everything I did to you",

" I was blind in revenge and never thought how I was destroying your life. Forgive me Jhanvi. Please ", he knelt on his feet and cried his heart out.

I wanted to console him, but I had lost trust. I turned around and moved into my room. He was in the guest room.

When there was nothing to say and show.

The next day at the breakfast table he didn't turn up. He had left for his hometown.

Next week Priya and Aunty visited me.

We all had a lovely time. I had the best time with them. Priya was in her trimester's.

Now they had the hint of our broken relationship.

" I know Jhanvi Rohit has hurt you a lot. He told us everything the day u left for Nagpur. But that has changed. He had become very sincere and left all his friends.

Now it's only me and him", said Aunty.

"Yes, bhabhie! You don't forgive him but give him a chance. Maybe he proves himself. In the end, your decision is a priority.", said Priya.

They left the next day.

I was in a dilemma about Rohit and forgiveness.

FOUR

NEW MOTIVE

There was chaos in Nagpur city. Sudden clashes between Hindus and Muslims. I had to leave for the office immediately.

Danish was my PA was waiting for all the details. DSP Ashutosh along with other officers were sitting in the meeting area.

We planned the routes and duties for the night and restricted movement in sensitive areas.

Officers left for their assigned task. Me and DSP stayed in for updates.

I told Danish to message sir that I would be able to come in the morning only.

Tea and coffee were arranged.

The whole night just passed with loads of tension. But everything went under control.

At 8 we met again and decided to follow the pattern for tonight with a little relaxation in the morning.

I left for home. It had been too hectic.

I had my breakfast with sir and mam, got fresh, and dozed off.

In the afternoon I was woken up by a Danish call. He asked me to come to the office immediately.

I got dressed up and rushed to the office.

As I reached the office there was a small girl of 1.5 years waiting with a doll in hand.

I entered my office. DSP addressed me

"Mam this child has been rescued after yesterday's clashes. Her mother was Muslim and her father was Hindu they Got married last year. They have been killed. They were the initial cause of the riots. Now the grandparents want the child. We have rescued her from the mosque."

I was shocked to hear the story. How can you kill people for honor of your caste, and pride?

Mob leeching is the latest trend to take revenge on people and get released on a social cause.

"Who are the people who mob leeched?

Both Religion or anyone grp.

I asked everyone to leave me alone for a moment. I called Danish and he told me.

Reem Sheikh and Arjun Mishra studied in the same college and soon became very good friends. We have checked their background Reem is the daughter of Raaes Sheikh the largest furniture chain in Nagpur.

Arjun's father is a government employee and has a very low profile. Just earning enough to complete their needs.

After college Arjun joined a firm as an accountant. He went to Reem's house with the marriage proposal and was rejected saying that they had fixed her marriage in Hyderabad.

Seeing that their parents were not ready to listen they ran away and married. They settled in Ahmedabad as Mr. And Mrs. Gupta. Reem's father had lots of connections in

1.5 years he traced their location. Leaders or I would say sanctimonious persona of our religion were outraged by their inter-caste marriage.

Raes Sheikh kept fuelling them now and then. When he came across their location he planned and started plotting to kill them.

They kept it a secret from Arjun's family.

Arjun and Reem were manipulated by her father. They told them that Arjun's mother was sick. Everyone had forgiven them and they should move back with their families.

Reem's father wanted to get Arjun killed and then get her daughter Nikah done.

But God had his ways. As they entered Nagpur they were attacked by a huge mob. Reem got serious head injuries while Arjun fled with her daughter.

Rae's plan was a complete failure.

He overreacted and killed the temple priest in the outrage. He doubted that Arjun was hiding there.

These Hindu-Muslim clashes started. Soon Arjun's family and community came out in his support and violence broke out. They entered the Masjid and destroyed Various parts.

"Get the culprits arrested asap. Danish"

"I want Rae's the mastermind"

I was loud and clear.

"Yes, mam. We are even looking for Arjun. Going through all the CCTV at roadside shops, bus stands, and stations.

We have even shared his pictures with rewards across the city", danish explained.

I asked to send the little girl to my room.

She came in with baby steps and I made her sit on the sofa. Danish brought in some biscuits and hot milk.

"Come here little one. What's your name", I asked the little one.

She was dressed in a pink dirty salwar suit. The hairs were all messed up. She had big protruding eyes and small pink lips.

I made her comfortable and ate something.

"My name is Sahiba. Where is my Ammi and abbu", she stammered in a feeble voice.

"They are in hospital they got hurt and are being treated", I lied to her.

She finished the pack of biscuits and milk. I made her lie down and soon she dozed off to sleep.

I called DSP.

"I want to take Sahiba with me. What are the proceedings? She is not safe anywhere. It's no age to lose ur parents", I said in a rage.

"Mam I will get the papers ready in an hour. You will be able to take her along mam."

He left the room.

30 years back it was a stormy night when I was travelling with my mom and dad. I was 5 years old. An overspeeding truck hit us and I lost my parents. I was taken by sister Agatha. For months I would ask her about my parents' newspapers for their whereabouts. Slowly I developed a habit of reading and writing. Sister Agatha started sending me to a convent school. Then I never looked back.

Today Sahiba reminded me of my childhood. I had been lucky to be with the best people and wanted the same for Sahiba.

By evening papers were ready and I took official custody of the child until the court decided. I also filed her adoption request.

We reached home after buying a few necessary clothes, toiletries, and toys.

She was now a little busy with her belongings. I had informed sir about arrival and he and mam were waiting.

As got down the car Juneja sir took her in his lap.

"Hello, little girl! I am your nanu", he smiled and shook hands with her.

Sahiba was very shy she hid her face under my arms.

Mam took her now and kissed her forehead.

"Such a beautiful baby, what's your favorite food? I will make one for u for dinner", she enquired.

Sahiba had never experienced so much love and attention she tried to hide her face in the teddy bear we just bought.

As instructed my room was adjusted for Sahiba to be along with me. We came I the room and she sneak-peeked from one corner to another.

"M I going to live here with you, where is Amma."

Her question perturbed me.

I brought her to my lap and sat on the bed.

"Did someone hit your mother and father?"

Her innocent face looked at me.

"Yes at night few men called Abba outside and then a few dragged Ammi out. I hid myself beneath the bed." She started sobbing and hugged me tight.

"Sahiba Ammi and Abbu are in hospital for treatment they will soon come to meet", again prevaricated Sahiba.

I made her decorate the room the way she wanted it to be. Her wardrobe, pillow, bed sheet, and of course the teddy bear and doll.

She carried the bear everywhere. Soon we joined for dinner. There was poori sabzi, especially for her and halwa at the end.

She had delectation in this home.

We all played Ludo and soon she dozed off to sleep.

I sat with Sir for her consultation as always. She applauded my act and was very proud. I told him I wanted to adopt her forever.

"Yes, it would be a blessing for the little one".

We too retired to our room.

Sahiba was sleeping with her bear. She had so much innocence in her face. These are angels of God.

Unaware of the loss they have incurred in life. I thanked God for another blessing from him.

The next day we got hold of people who had been responsible for this. They were both Hindu and Muslim leaders who joined hands to teach them a lesson.

Rae was also arrested, although he was guilty he made sure that he was punished.

They destroyed the small happy family of Sahiba. Her father was still missing.

I asked the DSP to teach them a good lesson and no leniency.

When on my way home I got some candies for Sahiba. She was elated to see me. We two sat down to tell each other what we did all day.

She becomes top of the town, yup top of the house.

Sir and Mam had a new task to wander around Sahiba and teach him different things.

I had ensured full Custody of Sahiba.

One day I had to call Rohit as well for his signature was required. I told him the complete sorry and he came in to sign the documents as my Husband and Sahiba's guardian.

The next day he spent the whole day with her. In 2-3 months. She had learned a few English and Hindi words. She would mix them and make her own.

She kept explaining things at her pace to Rohit. I was watching them from the room. Rohit was enlightened by her innocence.

I could sense a few visible changes in him.

Now he didn't bother me and appreciated my decision to adopt Sahiba.

He promised to be the best father. He stayed for a week and all four of them made a good team.

Soon Rohit left for home and asked me to come for Diwali.

I discussed with Juneja, sir. He too agreed with me.

"Yes he has changed now there is no arrogance. Just pure love for Sahiba. He didn't even question you, for his own child", said sir.

FIVE

FORGIVENESS

After a lot of thinking and suggestions from Juneja sir, aunty, Priya, and mam, I finally decided to visit Rohit's home for Diwali. I called Aunty and updated her on my program. We got our ticket confirmed as merely 5days leave had been sanctioned.

Big responsibilities in life make you sacrifice.

I had informed Sahiba that we would be traveling to the place for Diwali.

Juneja sir went to their home for Diwali. They had missed the place so much.

Jhanvi had decided to meet aunty and Priya. I was excited to take Sahiba home.

I had moved on in life. The rohit chapter was long closed. Now I endured this relationship just for Sahiba. I wanted to do things for our society and help more children like Sahiba to get a better life for a living.

Sometimes life has very strange ways of teaching us lessons and then we learn them for our whole life. Sahiba is a motive for me to do something for our society and change their perspective. Religious riots, mob leeching, allegations on each once culture and relic beliefs.

A day before Diwali I reached home.

To my surprise, it was decorated with ballons and flowers.

Rohit stood there with a huge teddy bear. Sahiba left my hold and rushed to Rohit. She jumped on her and Rohit caught hold of her. I could see a new bond between them.

Rohit had also realized his mistake and was mending it by giving unconditional love to Sahiba.

Everything at home had changed there were pictures of everyone Aunty, Priya, me Rohit, and even Sahiba were put up on a wall in the living area and it had had new decor. I reached my room and to my surprise, it had a big picture of all three of us. We had a bigger king-size bed for Sahiba to fit in with us.

There was a small pink table and chair. In the corner, there was a teddy bear wardrobe. I was flabbergasted.

Sahiba ran from one corner to another. Touching and exploring all things around her. She suddenly said

"Papa has made the home so beautiful Mom", she kissed me on the forehead.

Everything seems like a dream come true.

Soon she ran out to play with Rohit and her new friend Chikoo the Bear.

I settled down in my room and found a small note in my wardrobe.

"I regret my actions with you. I don't ask for forgiveness, because that's not possible I have made a mistake that can never be fixed. Your trust, love, faith everything was broken by me. You longed for family and love since childhood, I betrayed you completely.

It's just I want to be a father to Sahiba. She is the new ray of hope in my life. As if God has sent her to get rid of the sin I committed. I just request that let me be his true

father.

I plead with you Jhanvi."

Yes, Rohit had changed he was filled with remorse and guilt.

Today I feel Whom M I am as if god has created a bond of father and daughter.

God teaches us lessons for all our deeds.

www.ingramcontent.com/pod-product-compliance
Lightning Source LLC
LaVergne TN
LVHW040933150826
845672LV00007B/2346

* 9 7 9 8 8 9 6 3 2 0 1 5 9 *